TALES FROM THE GRANDFATHERS

Keith R. Carson

PITTSBURGH, PENNSYLVANIA 15238

The contents of this work including, but not limited to, the accuracy of events, people, and places depicted; opinions expressed; permission to use previously published materials included; and any advice given or actions advocated are solely the responsibility of the author, who assumes all liability for said work and indemnifies the publisher against any claims stemming from publication of the work.

All Rights Reserved
Copyright © 2019 by Keith R. Carson

No part of this book may be reproduced or transmitted, downloaded, distributed, reverse engineered, or stored in or introduced into any information storage and retrieval system, in any form or by any means, including photocopying and recording, whether electronic or mechanical, now known or hereinafter invented without permission in writing from the publisher.

RoseDog Books
585 Alpha Drive
Suite 103
Pittsburgh, PA 15238
Visit our website at *www.rosedogbookstore.com*

ISBN: 978-1-6442-6709-7
eISBN: 978-1-6442-6732-5

GRANDFATHERS

The Ancients, (Grandmother and Grandfathers) say that stories are to be shared so that knowledge in the Tribe can be increased, therefore it is with this in view that these stories are given to you the Reader/Listener. Stories float on the wind, for any one to tune into them. Some came by way of the Twisted Hairs, story- tellers who traveled the land, telling stories and sharing the ancient knowledge. Some stories come when this writer is siting beside the lake, discovering Water Woman, and other Spirit Helpers who share their stories and teachings. Others come because they (the stories) need to be told.

THE APPRENTICE

THE YOUNG GIRL WATCHED as the woman walked towards the woods through the lightly falling snow. She had been following the old woman since she left camp early this morning. Softly she walked; making sure her moccasin feet made no sound to give her position away. The old woman, wrapped in her shawl had entered the woods and was hidden from view. Quickly she covered the remaining distance and entered the pine grove too. The girl stopped and listened, she could hear singing ahead of her. She cautiously approached the sound.

It was the old woman. She was standing in the centre of a clearing in the Pines; she had dropped her shawl in the snow and had shed her loose garment to stand there clad only in her hair, which fell in greying strands to her waist. The old woman had her hands raised to the sky and was singing a song. Bright Feather listened; the words sent chills up her spine. The song was in celebration of the new snow and the time of winter when the land would sleep and gather strength for the new season to come.

The young girl thrilled to the melody, for it was a song borne out of celebration and love. It was a song from primal time; it was almost older than the hills themselves. The singing stopped, the old one turned. Bright Feather knew she had been seen because she was being motioned to come forward. The girl did as she was bidden. She walked toward the woman. She stopped the edge of a circle tramped in the snow. She had not seen it before but knew the woman had made it.

"Come into the circle with me Young One, but before you do, take all your garments off."

The girl did as she was told. Shivering in the coolness, she stepped into the circle and stood in front of the old woman.

"I am here to celebrate the coming of winter," the woman said, "why are you here?"

"I came because I must, I cannot stay away, please teach me" was the girl's reply.

After speaking the words Bright Feather realised that she was not cold inside the circle, even though the falling snow had melted on her shoulders and was running in small rivulets down her body.

"Good enough reason, I accept you as an Apprentice, and we will begin your training today. First we will begin with songs as they raise your Spirit up to meet the Higher Spirit coming down. But first I will tell you a story that was told to me when I began my apprenticeship. In the beginning – the Earth and Sky were One – there was no division. All the creatures and man lived in Peace and Harmony. In a far away land there were two brothers; they were called Cain and Able it was they who brought division to the land.

So began the training of Little Feather who later earned the Honor Name of Sky Dancer.
 HO, it is told.

DANCING FEATHER LEARNS A LESSON

Dancing Feather awoke from a troubled sleep. She could see that it was not yet dawn, as there was no light visible through the smoke hole of the teepee. Quickly she arose from her sleeping robes; donned her dress and picked up her moccasins and her belt knife. She lifted the tent flap and crept out taking care not to wake the family of sleepers within.

The air was cool and dark; the light of the beginning day was just touching the sky with its exploring fingers. She slipped the moccasins that her mother had made on her feet and shivered a little in the predawn cold. She wished that she had remembered her shawl but knew that she would not need it later in the day so she continued on her way toward the Medicine Woman's tent. As she approached the teepee, a figure detached its self from the tent shadow. Dancing Feather was always surprised when the woman came to meet her. It was said that the woman never slept and always knew what was going on around her. No one had ever been able to creep up on her. The young boys always tried their creeping skills out on her and had never been able to succeed. Even the older Scouts had occasionally tried, with the same success, but of course, none would admit that to anyone.

Today was a special day; the two of them were to go to a hillside some miles away to gather special leaves and roots for curing illnesses. Grandmother, which is what Dancing Feather called the old woman, had said that she would teach her the names and uses of the plants she was going to collect that day.

"Well little one, it took you long enough to wake today. I thought you would sleep till the whole camp wakened." The old woman said with a welcoming smile.

"Have I kept you waiting long?" Dancing Feather asked.

"No not long, let us go now." The woman said over her shoulder as she turned and strode off in the direction of the hills to the North.

It was a long walk and the old woman set a good pace. The sun was almost at midpoint, when they reached the river ford at the bottom of the steep hills. They sat down to rest in the shade of a tree, ate some dried meat and when they finished that, picked some ripe berries along the bank. They completed their meal with a long drink of water from a cool shallow spot. Dancing Feather waded in the water and was refreshed; for the heat of the day had found them before they reached the river; making them both very warm when they stopped to rest. Searching along the riverbank, they found a small pool in which to bathe completely. Then the two put on clean shorter garments of knee length material, which Grandmother produced from her bag. This would assist them in their climbing as they would be climbing the rest of the way.

"Come, it is time to begin." The Medicine Woman said and waved her hands in the general direction of the hills. As they climbed, Grandmother began the instructions of the proper preparation of self before gathering any healing roots, leaves or berries. "Always," she said, "one must prepare them selves to gather that which will help the people. One must reverently approach that which is being given as a gift from the Plant People – one must be ready to receive their gifts but only after proper Mental, Physical and Spiritual preparations. You must bathe, put on fresh clothing and approach your task with Right Thinking. And always with an air of expectation and thanksgiving for what you will receive." She went on.

"Thanking the Plants in advance for what you are going to receive, lets them know that someone has come who will have need of them and what they can do for others later. Then the plants can prepare themselves to attract your attention because they know what you will need to have in your bag, even before you do."

"How can that be?" queried Dancing Feather.

"The plants know my child, the plants know." was the woman's cryptic reply.

"It is the same for the digging, always a digging stick, never anything sharp and never a knife, which would sever the plants connection to Mother Earth; the root is as important as the plant. It holds the earth to it and therefore its healing properties are connected to the earth as they should be."

All afternoon they gathered plants, leaves and roots, each was named and its curing powers were explained. When their task was completed, they packed their collection into bundles, flung them over their shoulders and turned for home. They came down the hills and crossed the river more quickly than earlier in the day, even with the bundles they carried. Dancing Feather was tired when they neared the village, but she was buoyed by the thought that others of the village would see her return with the Medicine Woman, and that she was carrying healing articles with her. The village would then know that she was apprenticed to the Medicine Woman.

Dancing Feather always liked the Summer Camp, the way it was nestled in a group of trees that gave it shelter from the heat of the sun and the summer winds that came with stifling lack of air. This happened occasionally but the camps' location helped to lessen the problem when it did occur. It was a good camp, well situated, she thought. The girl noticed that the Old Woman had stopped suddenly, even though they were some distance from the camp. Then she too sensed it, something was wrong.

To the west of the camp, she could see that the horses were milling around and at the same time she saw that there were no guards visible.

"Tiehasna." Hissed the Old Woman, "Enemies"

Dancing Feather knew she was right. She dropped her bundle and started to run toward the village. As she ran, she opened her mouth and gave a long shrill cry. It sounded like a wounded hawk's cry, but much shriller and much longer. It was taken up by other women in the camp who were unsure why the alarm had been sounded, but knew that no one would make the alarm sound without good causes. She saw the warriors of the tribe coming out of their tents with their weapons in their hands looking for the Enemy.

Her task done, the girl turned back to the Medicine Woman, who had not moved from the place where she had stood when the alarm was given. She ran back to the woman, and told her to seek safety as she had seen a number of painted Warriors rise from the ground to her right. They were moving toward the still standing old woman. Dancing Feather ran as she had never run before. She reached the old woman as the warriors sighted the two of them. One raised His bow and shot an arrow at them. It landed behind the young girl. Dancing Feather reached the old woman, grabbed her by the arm and tried to pull her down to make less of a target, but it was no use, it was like trying to pull a mature tree down. The old woman was rooted to the spot. Dancing Feather turned toward the enemy warriors, and saw that they were retreating in the face of an impending charge by the men of the village, who had caught their horses and had formed a line on the edge of the trees. The enemy warriors turned and loped off toward their own hidden horses. No one wished to face a mounted enemy on foot if they could help it. One of the retreating warriors turned toward the women and fitted another arrow to his bow and fired it at the women, in reprisal for the warning they had given that aborted the attack. He ran off without looking to see if his arrow had found its mark.

Dancing Feather knew where the arrow was heading. She remembered that she had seen it in a dream prior to waking this morning. It was heading straight for Grandmother. She shouted for the old one to get out of the way, but it fell on deaf ears. The woman was standing with her eyes closed as if in a trance. In slow motion

Dancing Feather saw herself run forward and place herself in front of her teacher. The arrow found its mark, but it was Dancing Feather who took the impact of the arrow in its full flight. It knocked her to the ground, but it id not kill her, she saw it was lodged just beneath her left collarbone, in the flesh of the shoulder. She dimly saw the Medicine Woman kneeling over her.

"I saw it happen in a dream and lost confidence in myself and did not give you the warning earlier. I am sorry." the girl said and gradually lost consciousness. But not before she heard the Medicine Woman say, "You must trust your intuition child, someday your life may depend on it. I won't always be around to shield you, you know."

That is how Dancing Feather came to be known as, "She who protects." And was given the Honour Name of Telanda Yania "She who calls a warning to shield the Tribe. She learnt a valuable lesson that day of trusting her intuition and acting on it.

This story is told. Ho.

CORN PLANTING MOON

LITTLE FOX LEFT HIS CAMP EARLY that morning and made his way toward the hills to the East. He had been told to go there when he was ready to seek his Vision Quest. Every boy in the tribe at one time or another went into the hills for four days to spend time fasting, and drumming to seek his vision that would declare his entry into manhood and become part of his story in the days to come.

His Grandfather Daketa had told him how to prepare himself for the vision quest by fasting, bathing in the stream, taking only his drum and a simple breach clout which he would leave behind him at some point in his journey up the hill. And of course a shawl that his Aunt had made for him. He climbed the highest hill in the area after a journey of only a short time. He hung his breach clout in a tree branch below the brow of the hill and climbed the rest of the way up clad only in his hair and carrying his drum and shawl. He had selected the highest point in the surrounding hills as his Grandfather had told him to do, found a spot on the cliff face that looked out over the country of his people. He faced East as he had been instructed, because that is where knowledge came from. It was often referred to as the Eastern Doorway. He knew that the South represented many things, the Coyote who was sometimes known as the trickster. As well ones Childhood is represented by this doorway. To the West, was a powerful doorway, representing knowledge, and wisdom gained as one grew older. The North doorway was the door represented by Ancient Wisdom, from the old ones, the Grandfathers and Grandmothers who had gone on before. Settling himself, he began to drum and sing, calling on the Great Spirit to send him a power dream, send him information that would be important to him in a "good way", something that would improve the knowledge of the tribe. He asked that he be sent something that would benefit every one. This was the way his Grandfather had trained to perform his quest. All day and all night, he sang, danced and drummed. Asking always asking. He continued until he was exhausted, fell down, regained his strength, and began again. Day two passed in the same manner. He had gone without food and water before so the hunger did not bother him too much. On the third day, he thought he smelled his mothers cooking, but it was only something carried on the breeze up from the valley below where his people were camped. His lips were becoming dry now and it was becoming harder and harder to get up after he had drummed and danced himself into exhaustion. But he rose again and again, repeating the singing of supplication accompanied by the drumming and the dancing, always the dancing. On the fourth day it was getting late in the day, he had received nothing at all. He became discouraged, for how could he go back to the tribe and report that he had seen or heard nothing. It was a bad sign; his luck would not be good. Who would want to ask him to go on a raiding party or hunt with the men, if he had received nothing from the Ancients? At the end of the day, he sadly began to climb down from his vantage-point. Disappointment was clearly in his steps as he retraced them to where he had left his breach clout. He was feeling weak as he reached up to retrieve his garment hanging in the trees. He tipped over as he was steeping into his clothing, and could not get up. He drifted into a trance and heard a voice calling to him, urging him to follow the voice. He felt himself rise up, and looked down at himself lying on the ground. Then he was borne away by the wind to another cliff shelter where a man sat tending a small fire. He was greeted, by a nod of acknowledgement and motioned to sit by the fire across from the wizened old man. This is what the man had to say.

"It is the time of the New Moon, a time of the corn planting ceremony. This ceremony is as old as remembered time for us. Return with me, in your mind to the time of the Corn Planting Ceremony. We on the Plains have always held this ceremony to honour the planting which takes place on the New Moon in May.

This is how it was done. It is night and the New Moon as risen in the clear night sky, the camp fire burns brightly as the people circle the fire and sing the old songs of celebration for another growing season.

See the moon, hear the crackling fire, smell the smoke and hear again our people chanting their songs of celebration. Each person gives thanks for what they have received and in faith, plants again, in the expectation that the growing soon to come. The chosen maidens do their part in the fields, making their deposit, drawing the sacred symbols in the earth, while the Elders drum and sing their songs. The children listen to the old stories and the young men dream dreams of bravery and good deeds.

The Grandfathers and the Grandmothers tell the story of how the people of the Lakota Sioux were visited by the Moon Maiden who gave them the secret of the Corn and its planting. They were told how the plants should be tended and when the right time comes, the harvest may be taken from Mother Earth who nurtures us. The corn will sustain us through the long winter. As we eat we must always give thanks for that which we are given. We must learn to live in harmony and in doing so we will reap the harvest that is rightfully ours.

Thus we were told in the days of long ago. Therefore I say to you brothers and sisters remember this Corn Planting Ceremony, teach it to your children so that the planting will be done properly and so that the harvest may be taken at the proper time.

I am Shines in the Night Sky, and I give you this story so that you will not forget. You are entrusted with the ceremony of the planting, so that your harvest may be fruitful, when the time is right. Keep the legends and the ceremonies. Remember them well for they are your heritage and your obligation.

Ho, it is done."

Little Fox woke up he was lying under the tree where his clothing had hung. He was no longer dizzy he didn't even feel thirsty. He was full of joy. He had had his vision, had been given information for the tribe. Now he would be able to return to the tribe and report to his Grandfather, what he had heard. This is how Little Fox received his vision, returned to the tribe telling what he had been given. He was later named Corn Stalker and charged with looking after the Corn Planting Ceremony every year so that the harvest would be successful.

Ho!

THE BUFFALO WOMAN

The woman sitting in front of her tent looked up in disbelief why were these people giving her gifts? She felt that she had did not deserve what she was receiving. There were shawls, moccasin's, and garments with fine beadwork, all manner of things including baskets, tools and meat. Each gift was being laid at her feet with Reverence and Awe.

As she looked around the camp, the dust still had not settled from the passing of the Buffalo herd. The woman reasoned that she had only done what she thought was necessary, anyone else would have done it as well. She recalled what had happened earlier in the day.

She had come out of her morning meditation and knew that the village was in grave danger. She hadn't known what the danger was, only that she knew about it and therefore had to do something about it. She knew what direction the danger would come from and that is all she knew. Getting up from the floor in the teepee she went out of the camp to the East and stood at the edge of the perimeter that marked the beginng of the camp and waited.

Many people of the tribe saw her standing there hour after hour, singing and holding her rattles toward the sky. They wondered in a curious way what she was doing, but thought that Medicine People were always doing strange things.

Time passed, it was late afternoon, Thunderclouds could be seen in the East and the occasional flash of lightning was visible. Then everything around the camp seemed to grow still; even the children stopped their playing. Then a low rumble could be heard in the hills from an easterly direction, the rumble got louder and louder, then the ground began to shake. The people became frightened, they knew it was the buffalo in stampede and there was nothing they could do to stop a herd once it had begun to move. The villagers began to run wildly about in the camp, some trying to catch horses on which to ride to safety. Others began to strike their tents but each knew in their hearts that flight would be useless – where would one run to on the prairie? Closer and closer came the herd, the camp horses became terrified and broke away from their tethers, the dogs ran away in terror. Mothers hid in their tents and covered the children. Some warriors took their bows and moved out toward the oncoming sound, thinking that perhaps they could turn the herd by killing the lead element. There was not enough time to organize, when the first wave of the animals broke over the rolling hills a half a mile away and ran straight toward the camp. All this time, the Medicine Woman held her ground at the perimeter of the camp, no one could have reached her in time to save her and elude the thundering herd at the same time.

Closer and closer they came. The wind brought the sound of the snorting, roaring terrified herd to the villager. The Medicine Woman had stopped singing, and had bowed her head in prayer, rattles hanging limply at her sides. In a minute the villagers realized that the herd would over run the woman's position. Those with courage looked to see the brave woman's last minutes. But the herd did not run over her – instead it split in two, each division of the split went around her in an ever increasing "V". Each side of the separation bypassed the sides of the village. The noise of the herd was terrible; no one could hear their own voice, even if they had uttered a sound.

Some say it was the largest herd they had ever seen or heard of in the stories given to the people. It completely missed the village, no one was harmed; not one teepee was damaged. All were safe. No one knows how the woman did it, and no one ever attempted to duplicate the feat!

The Elders say they saw a White Buffalo standing behind the woman; others say there was too much billowing dust to see anything. What is certain is that the woman turned the herd, by Power, Magic, Spirit Helpers or some other method, who can say? The deed had been done, no one could dispute that.

At the celebration fire that night, buffalo meat was thrown into the fire in thanksgiving and none was eaten. Chief Two Eyes proclaimed that the woman Medicine Woman would be given two new names. She would be called she who has the White Buffalo Woman for her protection and her Honor Name would be - Na Wellia Netawaw - "She who turned the herd on her own".

And so it was that the tribe, dwelling on the fringes of the High Prairies, came to have their own powerful protection of the White Buffalo Woman. Great were her honours and much honour she brought to the tribe over the years. And the Buffalo never ever stampeded close to the tribe again.

It is spoken. Wa Ho!

HIGH PLAINS TALKER

No one knows how the bitterness started between the two tribes, they only knew it had divided them for many a season, as far back as any one could remember.

The situation grew worse and worse between the tribes that year, and reached a high point when the tribes met at the yearly summer gathering. Neither Chief was willing to accept the campsites that had been chosen for them by the gathering Elders. Because the two angry tribes would be too close together and there campfire smoke would be in the nostrils of the other. Each Chief drew away from the other tribe to confer with his own Elders, on the matter and decide what they should do. Again the conflicting Chiefs met with the gathering Elders, and asked for a different campsite. One tribe to the North of the gathering and the other

Chief requested a site to the South. It seemed reasonable, but the Elders pointed out that if the sites occupied, their location would block the escape exits of the other tribes, should they be attacked. Neither Chief would bend in their resolution not to be located close to the offending tribe. It was decided to wait a little longer, and see if time would heal the rift. Each Chief withdrew to confer with his Elders.

The Chief, who had been given the northern site, was an impatient man, who had the pressure of his women to reckon with. They wanted to get the camp set up so that their daughters could begin looking for suitable mates from the neighbouring tribes, and thus increase the tribes numbers. How could they do that when their camp was not properly set up? Was the clammer from the women? The decision was made to set up camp in the Southern site, rather than the North one. But when the Chief and his tribe arrived, the offending tribe already occupied the site. They too had decided to go ahead with their set up in spite of the advice and wishes of the Gathering Elders.

Each tribe saw that the other had come to occupy the site. A call went out from the Southerly Tribe; it was the call of an "Enemy Alert", a call to War. The call was immediately answered by the Northern Tribe, the too sounded the enemy alert and their warriors moved out on the plain and prepared for battle. This show of force was met by an equal show of force from the southern tribe.

And that's how it stood, the warriors were ready for battle, each side drawn up in a line facing the other on the flat of the plain. This had never happened before at the summer gathering, at least in memory of any one who was there.

No one knows how it happened or where he came from but a man on a huge Medicine Horse rode out of the assembled groups of tribes gathered on the edge of that plain. He rode into the centre of the line between the two tribes and stopped his horse. He held up a ceremonial pipe he carried in his hands. He pointed the pipe at the four directions the horse turning as each motion began to the proper direction of North, East South and West. Then the motion of the pipe to the Earth and to the Sky and then in a circle to include all the People. The man jumped off his horse for an instant, reverently laid the pipe on the ground and sprang up on the animal again. Now the horse seemed to move of its own accord, for it had no rope or thong bridle that anyone could see. No one had ever seen such a display of horsemanship before. The horse and ride moved as one. The rider stood on the horse, at the back, the front and the middle while the horse moved at a full gallop between the two opposing tribes.

The rider swooped down, gathered his pipe up in his hand, rode toward the northern tribe and still at the full gallop, swooped down and placed the pipe on the ground in front of the tribe. He rode his horse a little way off from that tribe and then turned and rode straight at the line of warriors. The line of gathered ponies bent and gave way as the man bore down on them. The rider scooped up the pipe and turned his horse toward the Southern tribe. The same performance was repeated there. When the rider had retrieved his pipe, he rode out to between the two lines again. He stopped; then the horse made the recognized sign for talk. First walking to the left in a sidestepping motion, and to the right. The man made the Plains sign to signify that he would talk.

Each tribe on the plains has a slightly different language, but there was a common sign language developed over the years so that there would be no misunderstanding between tribes. Each tribe had a person who was trained as a Talker or Signaler who could sign and interpret the High Plains language. They were called to the front of the two tribes so that what the man on the horse was going to say could be correctly interpreted.

The story has been told and retold around many a campfire down through the years, this is what he said. "The Great Spirit gave this land to the People, to tender and care for. The land in return would care for us and tend to our needs. We have been told from earliest times, to live in harmony with Nature and it will live in harmony with us. It is certain the North and South tribes have somehow forgotten that they must care and tend to the needs of each of the other tribes. For is this not our sacred trust? We cannot spill the blood of a kinsman tribe. Mother Earth would be offended if we did this. Is this not so? If we war amongst ourselves, are we not diminishing the trust given to us? If we war between ourselves, remember we will be killing our brothers. Does not the male of one tribe join his bride's tribe? Are we not therefore all related? If we war against each other, we do not insure that the tribes increase because there will be two less tribes to choose eligible mates from? This is a beautiful day. How can we offend Father Sky by having him look down upon us fighting among ourselves? Would the Hawk make war against another Hawk? No, it is not in his nature to do that. I speak to both the tribes. Stop, sit down in counsel and try to discover w3hat it is that has separated both of you. If you cannot find what it is that separated you, then the difference is of no consequence. Therefore, Spirit commands that you lay down your arms, and embrace each other in harmony and brotherhood as men were meant to do. I have spoken," Having spoken the word in sign; the horse and rider turned and disappeared into the crown that had gathered on the edge of the plain.

Later, when the tribes had settled their differences and had made the sacred smoke together. They asked around to see who the man on the Medicine Horse was. No one knew no one had seen him in any of the tribes. Some say that they saw him on the edge of their tribal camps in the cold of winter sitting on his Medicine Horse looking in the direction of their camp. Others say he came to their camps to warn of danger, or to lead them to game when it was scarce on the land. No one doubted that he was looking after them, but no one ever found where he had come from.

Strange as it may seem, no one tried to give the man a name. He was just known as the Talker or the Rider of the Medicine Horse. Through the years, they heard of the man appearing in times of tribal need, rendering assistance and then disappearing again. Boys guarding the Horses claimed to have seen him on the edge of their camps, sitting on his horse, watching, just watching.

So it is told. Ho!

THE HELPERS

AFTER THE EARTH CHANGES, when the earthquakes had subsided and men once again began to live in harmony with his surroundings, there were numerous stories told around the fires of the Remaining People. Some were about the Marauders who came and vandalized everything. Taking what they wanted and destroying the rest so that on one else could have it. The story goes; that a group defeated these marauders, that seemed to know their every move. But that's another story to be told at another time.

Our story concerns something that the Remaining People told; about receiving help from a group of people that would appear out of nowhere, render assistance. Even staying until the trouble passed and then the Helpers as they became know, would vanish, leaving behind only those who had been helped to tell about what they had received.

I my self, as old as I am, received help from the Helpers and I would like to tell you about it if I may. I had been hunting far from our main camp during the early winter. I had tracked some game into a forest, but lost the trail when it began to snow in one of those quick line squalls that sometimes spring up without warning. I was angry with myself for losing the trail and angrier at getting myself into a predicament where I was beginning to doubt that I would make it into a safe shelter. It was snowing hard, and I lost sight of the landmarks that I had taken note of on my way into the forest. The wind came up and made forward progress even worse. I decided to den up for the day and wait the storm out. I looked around for some suitable shelter but could only find an overturned tree whose roots and the surrounding dirt would provide me with some shelter from the wind.

I managed to build a small fire but my situation was getting worse. I was loosing my body heat and was getting colder and colder. Then I heard a noise in the storm, at first I couldn't make it out, by straining my ears, I managed to catch what it was. It was a voice saying, "Hello, Hello." In the middle of a raging storm, you can imagine that it was an eerie sound. Naturally I answered back. "Hello, I am over here." The voice and I exchanged hellos for a time, and then a shape emerged from the storm to stand in front of me. It was a man completely wrapped in furs carrying a long stick. He told me that his camp was not far from where we were and that I was welcome to share his shelter. Of course I accepted, for I knew I was doomed out in the cold where I was. He turned, beckoned me to follow him and strode off into the storm, his retreat was so fast that I barely had time to put out the fire and follow him before he was lost in the swirl of the falling snow.

We tramped for quite a while, with me never letting the man out of my sight because of his swiftly moving gait. Lord only knows where we were, as I had no idea at all, but the man seemed to know where he was going. So I just followed along. It appeared that we were travelling in a straight line, but the senses can be deceiving in snow blinding conditions. We forged on through the storm for what seemed hours, which in reality was only a short time. I sensed rather than saw the campsite, as the ground was cleared and flat. The striding man slowed his forward progress imperceptibly. Out of the snow, I saw it; a cabin nestled snugly under a hillside. There was smoke coming out of the chimney and as small light in the window. The man stopped, gave a long low whistle and knelt down in the snow. A dog came from the cabin and ran toward him. The man ruffled its fur and turned and motioned me forward. The man appeared to say something to the animal and held out his hand for mine. I held it out and the dog smelled it. Satisfied, the animal turned toward the cabin and trotted off. The man and I moved toward the cabin as well. Once inside we hastened to rid ourselves of our outer garments and were soon crouched beside the stone fireplace warming ourselves up. When I had warmed up a bit, I began to look around. There were three others in the cabin besides the man. A young woman and two older ones. The young woman brought me a steaming bowl with some stew in it. The taste was delicious, doubly so because I had not eaten for most of the day. Sitting by the fire, I felt myself being regarded by the man. The others were regarding me as well; I thought it best to tell them that I was Lemo, Chief Hunter for our group. The man told me that his name was Phillip and then introduced me to the others. One of the older women had white hair, she was call Whin, and the other older one was called Mar, while the younger woman was called Cala. The dog was affectionately introduced as Woof. The man explained the reason the dog was call Woof, was because he didn't bark.

Looking around the cabin I could see that they were prepared for winter, they had provisions hanging from hooks in the ceiling beams and there were baskets stored near the back of the cabin and under the sleeping benches. Hanging on pegs behind the door were outer garments for each of the inhabitants and robes were piled on the sleeping benches in the back. I was still hungry but thought it impolite to ask for more food. But one of the women got up from the corner where she had been sitting, took my bowl from my hand, refilled it and handed it back to me. It was uncanny, almost like they were reading my mind. Now that I thought of it, they didn't appear to speak very much. The man asked me if I was tired, and I told him that I was. He showed me a place to lie down, gave me a robe which to cover my self with and before the robe reached my shoulders, I was sound asleep. It had been a long day.

When I woke up the next morning, there were only three people in the cabin. The young woman was gone. The man greeted me when it was apparent that I was awake. He asked me if I would like some heated biscuits and some tea for breakfast. I told him that I would. Our breakfast finished, I asked the man where we were. He indicated that we were somewhere miles up river from my camp. I had no idea that he knew the whereabouts of my camp, he replied that they knew where all the camps were in this region. When I questioned him on how he knew their locations, all he did was smile. When I pressed him for an answer he just looked at me. That is when I noticed his eyes, they were green, but they had deepness to them as well as a spark of vitality that was astonishing. The eyes once you looked at them were so kind and gentle. I had seen that look once when a father looked at his child whom he was proud of. The look really puzzled me, it really did.

The man and I worked all day beside the fire, on some leather he was tanning. He told me that it was still blowing and snowing out and that it would be impossible for me to go back to my camp that day. So we worked. Toward the end of the day, just before it got full dark the man said to no in particular, "Cala comes." He asked me to put on my outer garments and go outside to help him. Once outside, could see that he had been right, it was still snowing and blowing. Again the man strode off into the swirls with me following close behind him. This time the dog came out of the snow swirls to greet us and lead us up the hill behind the cabin. There struggling to navigate through the snow was Cala and some one she was half carrying, half dragging like an awkward stack of wood. Quickly the man and I took the person under each arm and supported the barley walking figure as we made our way back to the cabin. Once inside, Cala and the other women brought the fur wrapped figure to the fire. When the outer garments were stripped away we discovered a woman underneath. She was slightly delirious, she kept raving about something, but it was hard to tell what it was she was saying. We figured out what it was when Cala unwrapped herself from her outer garments and I noticed that she had a baby slung to her front. The woman must have been afraid for her baby.

Each of the two new guests were made more comfortable by the fire, which revived the woman long enough to determine that her baby was safe before she lapsed into a sleep where she lay by the fire. She was gently carried to a bed and covered over with robes. The baby seemed to be all right, as it made no sound at all. It soon nestled beside her mother and fell asleep after satisfying itself at her breast.

The woman remained in the state of sleep for almost two days, rousing herself only long enough to satisfy herself that she was safe and that the babe was safe as well. It was a time for us, as we had to make room for the woman and her child who occupied the sleeping platform I had had. This made it necessary for me to sleep on the floor near the fire. But I had slept in worse places, so the prospect was not too objectionable. When she did finally rouse herself, the woman told us that she had been captured by a warring tribe and was being herded to their war camp when she managed to slip away. She eluded her captors when the storm came up but was unable to find suitable accommodations so she decided to continue her journey. She became lost in the blowing snow and did not remember too much about her wanderings except that she felt like lying down to sleep in the snow. She knew that sleeping was a bad thing so she kept going. The woman, whose name was Dana, could not remember too much about being found by Cala, she remembered giving her the baby and telling her to save the child. We soon learned that Dana had lain with a man she liked and some of the women did not like the liaison, so they had fabricated a story about Dana and some Sacred articles the women had stolen from the Medicine Tent. That was why she had been sent away from her tribe and had been taken by the war party. At one time the women wanted to make her abort the baby, by having the Medicine Woman give her a drink that would cause the fetus loss. The woman fought that idea and decided to carry the baby to term. You will learn that it was a good idea to birth the baby because the child was the one legends will be told about ... but I get ahead of myself.

We seven lived in the cabin for the remainder of the winter, getting to know each other and working harmoniously as a small cell. Naturally when Spring came I returned home to my tribe. By then Dana and I had become friends, I liked her and she like me; so she came home as my woman. The baby lived with us through her growing years and became one of the most powerful Medicine Women in remembered history. But that's another story. One thing that was never explained to me was how the group in the cabin knew Dana or myself needed help or how to find us. When I asked any one of them, they would just smile and say; "you will know one day, if you are meant to do so." I discovered how they did it, when years later, I hurt myself far from camp and Dana came to me and healed my leg. When I asked her how she knew that I was hurt, she said that she had heard me call in her dreams and knew where to look for me.

Later on when I went back to search for the cabin, it was gone. The four were not there either but we heard of their deeds elsewhere from time to time. Then Dana and would look at each other and smile because we knew that the helpers had cared us for too.

MIRACLE ON THE PLAINS

Tell me my friend
Where were we when we turned our horses South
And rode into the wind?
Each alone with his thoughts of the sights and sounds he had witnessed.
Tell me my friend, where were we when we turned our horses South and rode into the Wind?

THE SKY WAS INKY BLACK, punctured by a myriad of stars as Runs with Bears made his camp in a little depression. He built a fire and sat down beside it and thought about the last few days. He had been travelling toward the East, always toward the East. He was driven; he knew that and wondered what would happen next.

He was a Shaman of his tribe, who three days before, had ridden out of camp on his war pony. He had been driven out of camp by an incessant voice in his head. The voice kept saying, "come East toward the Rising Sun, there you will find the answers that you are seeking". He could not think of what the questions were that would require him to travel east at the beginning of winter, the beginning of the cold season. This was when everyone stayed near their camps and rested. Why was he out here, what was it that Spirit wanted him to learn? Always it had been the same, Holy Men in the tribes were those set apart. They were the ones that sought answers to questions posed by the tribe. But try as he might, he could not think of anything that he had consciously sought an answer for. It was puzzling, but that's what he always liked, something to think about. His wife said that he thought too much and one day it would waste his brain away. He doubted that very much. Once he solved this puzzle, there would be others. There always were.

He roused himself from his reverie; his ears had picked up a noise brought to him by the small breeze blowing from the North. What was it? A horse or some other animal. He quickly strung his bow, withdrew into the shadows away from the fire and waited. An accented voice called out. "I am alone, and wish to share the hospitality of your fire". If the voice spoke the truth, then Runs with Bears was obligated to grant the request. He replied to the voice. "If you are alone and mean me no harm then come in and share the fire". He heard someone alight and saw a man come into the firelight. He was a tall man, dressed in winter furs carrying a coup stick. The man sat down by the fire and held his hands out to the blaze. Runs with Bears stood up and walked to the fire, and stopped when he was opposite his guest. He spoke, "I am Runs with Bears, Shaman to the Eton Sioux to the West of here". The stranger introduced himself by saying. "I am Holy Man of the Ogala Sioux, I come from the North, my name is White Cloud". Runs with Bears invited the man to sit and warm himself. Etiquette demanded that the guest is given the first opportunity to speak, but Runs with Bears, decided to dispense with formalities.

"Can you tell me why you are out here on the Plains at the beginning of winter, are you lost?"

"No, not lost, just looking for something" was the reply.

"What do you mean?"

"It is strange, but four days ago, I was awakened in the night. I heard a maiden's voice singing in my ear. She said, over and over again. "Come out onto the plains, there I will reveal to you a thing of wondrous beauty. A thing so marvellous that you will scarcely believe it yourself." I left the camp and travelled in the direction that the maiden indicated to me. She has been singing in my ear every night since I left camp. Always the same song, but this evening the song was stronger, and kept urging me on. So I did not camp, I just kept travelling and here I am. And what about you?" He motioned to Runs with Bears.

After Runs with Bears told him his story, White Cloud said that it was a good story and offered a pipe to smoke. Both of them smoked in a ceremonial way until the pipe was gone. Each maintained his silence; each was lost in thought. Before they rolled in their robes they tied their ponies to their legs with long braided thongs. They agreed to travel together since they believed they were seeking essentially the same thing. Each man drifted off to sleep with their voices keeping them company.

In the morning, they agreed that they should continue to the East as each had heard in their dreamtime, the instructions to do so. It was a cold morning, promising sunshine and warmth later in the day as they turned their horses toward the rising sun and rode away from their camp. The two men travelled together for three days, always east, and always with the voices accompanying them. Each learned more about their travelling companion. Each told the story of their Medicine Dreaming, their Hunts, their battles and how they each came to be Medicine Men for their tribes. They enjoyed each others company and found that they shared many interests in common. Runs with Bears was an excellent shot with the bow and brought down small birds and rabbits for their evening meal. White Cloud always succeeded in starting a fire with his fire making tools on the first try, so he took on that duty each time they made camp. They found the occasional dry tree or dried Buffalo chips with which to make a good fire to cook their meat. Each had other dried provisions that they shared. It was a good travel.

As they moved East across the land, they saw no one else. Even the winged ones were not as frequent as they usually were no Hawks or Eagles dotted the fast panorama sky. On the evening of the third day, they had settled in the camp, eaten their meal and were sitting by the fire when they heard bells in the still air. Each moved away from the glow of the fire and waited. The bells came closer and closer. A man rode into the firelight. He too was dressed in winter furs and carried a long decorated ceremonial stick. He spoke to each of them. "I am called Hunts Wisely, I am Hunkpapa of the Lakota Sioux, I come alone, and I come in peace". White Cloud and Runs with Bears invited the man to come to the fire and share it with them.

When Hunts Wisely had warmed himself by the fire, he told his story. He said that he had been travelling for a hand plus two. He had been driven out of his camp by the voice of a Brave, telling him it was time to travel the open land, time for him to see a wondrous sight and time for him to marvel at the honour given to few men. It was for him to come to see and then carry this tale back to his people. Hunts Wisely said that the Brave directed him when to go, when to stop and where to turn next. It was a good way to go, to be able to follow the voice. The voice said it would guide him and also keep him safe. That is why he rode right into camp, because the voice told him that it was safe to do so. Again the men smoked and thought about what each had revealed about their own stories. They agreed to travel together to see what would the next days would bring. They took to their robes and slept.

Each of the men woke at the same time, not quite knowing why. Then they realised that the sky was brightly lit. Each knew that it was not dawn, but something was different. Then they heard it, the sound of drums, and voices singing. It was unlike no other singing that they had ever heard. There were also other strange instruments playing as well, wind instruments and reed pipes. The singing voices went right through each men and the melody seemed to lift them up out of their robes until they were standing at different points around their camp fire. Then they saw who was doing the drumming. It was a gathering of men and women standing around a central figure. The singing was the most marvellous that the men had ever heard. Then they realised that the gathered people were not on their level, these singers were in the sky. They were suspended in the sky there was no ground under their feet. They were just suspended within a great light that completely filled the sky.

As they listened to the Singers, they realised that they were not all the same colour, some were Red, like themselves and some were Black, there were others who were White and still others who had skin with a Yellow hue. When they listened they heard the combined group singing a welcome song; welcome to He Who Is Our Elder Brother. Then the central figure detached itself from the group and floated down to where the men stood. It was a man dressed in fine white buckskin, decorated in a pattern none of the men had ever seen. Then they noticed that the Man was not only a Man but was a Woman as well. They marvelled at this new aspect before them. The two people stood side by side and began to speak in unison.

"Greetings to you Three, we come from the Great Spirit, we are the male and female manifestation of Him who sent us." As they spoke their faces changed colour to match the colour of the peoples they had seen in the air. " We bring you good news. This day in a village far away called Bethlehem is born a man-child. He is called Jesus, Emmanuel, and the Great Peacekeeper. To the people of the Plains he shall be called The Dawn Star, Elder Brother, and Pointer of the Way. This shall be the sign to you. He will come bearing a tree that the tribes will use as a healing herb. It will be called Cedar. It will be many seasons before he shall come your way. But come he shall. Your people will face many trials and almost complete destruction before the peoples of the East and those here on the Plains can walk in Peace with their other brothers from the four directions of the compass. But it will come. The time will come when all can walk in Peace and harmony. When men and women and children are free to seek their destinies and develop their talents in a way that is pleasing to the Great Spirit. A time when all can walk in Peace with no fear of danger in their coming and goings. But that time is far ahead. You three are charged with the telling of the news that we bring you and the promise that we give you here and now. This is our promise and our pledge to you. Take the message and spread it among your tribes and to all the peoples of this land. This is your mission, this is your destiny this is your duty to the tribes every where. Do not fear for your safety, you will be welcomed everywhere, we will go before you to the wise men and women of each tribe to prepare the way. You will be provided for in the way that you need to be. Act on our advice and our counsel and no harm will come to you ever. We charge you do this thing in the name of Him Who Sent Us. As it is told, let it be done. Ho."

Then the two forms blended into one and retreated into the sky. The gathering of men and women began to fade and the light receded with them. The singing was heard for some time, then there was silence. A silence so still that each man felt the moisture in the air as if it were rocks along a river bed, and it carried with it a presence of great intensity and strength. The smell of wood smoke hung heavily in the air, but there had been no campfires. Each men knew in his heart that what he had seen was real and not something he had imagined. They felt that the presence surrounding them was nurturing and comforting and strengthening all at the same time. They each knew that they were impervious to harm. They knew all things, they heard with new ears, saw with new eyes and felt with new hearts. They knew they were part of the presence and that the presence was part of them. They were all and all were One.

They stood rooted to the spot for a long time after the light had subsided and the singing stopped. None knew how long. When they finally took stock of their surroundings they noticed that their clothing had changed, each was dressed in fine Ceremonial Dress with mystical beadwork woven into the clothing. They each had high moccasins on and there was an Eagle Feather wand at their feet. They also noticed that their hair had turned white, and was plaited in a braid, which hung over their left ears. They also noticed that each was marked with an animal on their foreheads. The man from the North had a Bison, the Man from the South had a Wolf and the man from the West had a Bear as his tattoo. Each of them could communicate with the other without speaking, each knew his Brothers' thoughts, as his was known by the others. Each man agreed that they had seen something marvellous and that they would carry the tale to their tribes and that each would hand the information down through the generations until the message came to fulfilment as the two who were one gave it that night.

When they departed the camp, they rode South with each other until it was time to turn in their own direction. Each turned away from the other, but they knew that they would always be in contact with each Brother and that they would fulfil the mission that was given to them and that the message would be carried to the tribes and kept until the prophesy would come to fulfilment. It was a good travel; they would fulfil their Destinies as it was given to them. That is why the message is still there with the tribes. Shaman and Holy Men have passed down the message from generation to generation. They await the fulfilment of the Prophecies that were given that night. Soon, soon, it will come to pass.

Tell me my friend - where were we when we turned our houses South and rode into the wind. Where were we? HO it is spoken.

THE COMING OF THE HORSE TO THE LACOTA SIOUX

It was a time of story telling around the campfires in the evening. Daola a Grandfather stood up to speak. He cradled the Talking Stick in the crook of his left arm. All were silent to hear his words, even the young children knew that he was a powerful dreamer. It was good medicine to be touched by his words. "I had a dream last night," he said. "In that dream I saw our warriors as half men and half beasts. They were men from their heads to their waists then they were four legged beasts with shaggy coats and long tails. They could run like the wind. The warriors who were half men and half beasts surrounded the buffalo herd; they fired many arrows and made many kills. Some of our warrior-beasts were killed as the buffalo herd stampeded. They were ground into the dust under the hooves of the buffalo. But their hunting deeds did not go unnoticed. They were mighty hunters. They brought much food to the tribe.

These warrior-beasts could cover long distances and take our warriors scouting into country that would have taken a long time to cover. Now they did it in half the time it takes to tell about it. I saw some of these warrior-beasts pulling long sticks behind them with the village tents and other supplies piled on top. Whole villages could be moved with ease. No more camping in the open until we had taken hides to make our tepees. Now our tepees went with the tribe. When we moved all our possessions went with us. The sick and feeble could be taken with us and not left alone on the trail to die as before. Our contact with Brother and Sister tribes would be made easier because we could travel more swiftly. News of other camps would reach us faster. Traders would come bringing more goods to trade. In time these warrior-beasts would become a sign of wealth among our people. So too would the taking of these warrior-beasts become a sign of courage and prowess among our warriors. What better way to demonstrate your skill at stalking and tracking than to take what our enemies have for ourselves? Skill in capturing and training these warrior-beasts would become an honoured place in our tribe's circle of skills. Soon everyone will come to know these animals very well. We will wonder how we ever did without them. I saw these warrior-beasts coming up from the South where they are even now reaching Turtle Island. This a true rendition of my dream."

So spoke the old man of his dream that night around the campfire. All marvelled at his story and some thought his tale the ramblings of an old man. Others said that what he had seen other times came true, therefore there was no reason to doubt what he had to say that night. Some wondered what these warrior-beasts would be called. Others thought his tale very far into the future. Others spoke of tales of a new race of people coming to visit who were pale in the face, spoke a different language and carried weapons that could kill at a greater distance than the best bowman ever had. Who could this new race be? What had they to do with the warrior-beasts?

So many thoughts were carried to bed after the campfire that night.

There was one boy who had heard the words of the old man and it had fired his imagination. Spotted Elk resolved to be the first one to see these animals and to learn to tame and use the animals. He desperately wanted an honoured place in the tribe and saw the warrior-beasts as his way of making a name for himself and claiming his place in the history of the tribe. He curled in his blankets and fell instantly to sleep. To dream of warrior-beasts, himself, other tribes and an adventure beyond his wildest dreams...

HO!

GRAND FATHER SPEAKS

It is the time of the Summer Rendezvous. A time for connected sub-tribes to reconnect with their distant kin - a time for marriages to be made - a time for young men to have their Vision quests - and a time to have these quests interpreted by wise men of the Whole Counsel, this is one of these stories.

Outside the grand circle of teepees sits a teepee - alone - with smoke curling lazily from the smoke hole - a young man approaches.

This is what happens; scratching is heard on the teepee door flap. a soft voice is heard to say "come in"

Boy   "greetings grandfather" as he enters the door and closes it behind him.

G/F   What can I do for you?

Boy   I have been on a Vision Quest and seek interpretation to what I have seen.

G/F   Did you fast for the required three days?

Boy   I did Grandfather

GF   Did you climb to a high spot

Boy   Yes, it was a long climb but I made it

G/F   Did you anything with you except a shawl?

Boy   No, and the shawl was a gift from my Mother Yellow Moon

G/F   Did you sing to the Spirits to help and guide you?

Boy   yes - but my voice gave out on the third day

G/F   That is to be expected

Boy   May I tell you what I saw on the fourth day after I thought I had not succeeded - I gave myself up to the Spirits - it is then that I saw.

G/F   What did you see my son?

Boy   I saw an animal that was like a Buffalo - but not a Buffalo it was tall had a long tail and a head that was larger still - big eyes and a nose bigger than a Buffalo - I saw myself riding on the back of this animal. I carried a lance and was leading warriors into battle.

A long pause

G/F   What else did you see or hear?

Boy   I saw a black animal like a mountain lion, but not a mountain lion. It spoke to me.

G/F   What did this animal say to you?

Boy   He said I was chosen to lead my tribe to victory. I was chosen to be a wise man and to lead with grace and wisdom - to be a friend to widows and orphans and I would be able to give wise counsel because I listened to counsel from the Spirits. And not to make hasty decisions.

A long pause ensued

Again G/F spoke - what else happened?

Boy   a hawk settled on my shoulder and said "greetings - from now on you will be known as Grey Eagle. The Spirits have spoken"!!

G/F   What did you feel?

Boy   It is strange you should mention that. I felt a huge shiver up my back and the hairs on my arms stood up after the Hawk had spoken his words to me.

G/F Any thing else?

Boy Yes. Four wolves came and sat around me. They sat around me in each of the four directions. One spoke to me and said, "we will be with you everywhere when you travel. We will surround you and act as your travelling companions. We will give you joy on your travels.

G/F What else did you notice?

Boy It is strange that you should ask that question. I had forgotten this, but as soon as you mentioned it I recalled seeing two more other animals - a huge Moose with a very large and wide set of antlers. He walked through my space. Also a Doe Deer followed the Moose.

G/F Anything else?

Boy After my vision when the two animals went away, I lingered for a long time - but did not feel time going by. Then I stood up, I felt light headed and discovered that I had grown taller. I also noticed my muscles had grown larger, as well, I felt changed. I was a boy no longer, I was a MAN!! I thought like a man, I stood as a Man, I walked like a Man, and I WAS a MAN a hunter, a warrior, AND ready to be a husband because I knew intuitively where to go to steal horses as a Bride Price for the girl who would be my woman.

A longer pause ensued

Then Grandfather spoke - are you ready to hear the interpretation - knowing that much of what you have experienced is to be kept to yourself and not to be shared with anyone.

    This is your Medicine and gives you power - reveal it and your power will be weakened with the telling.

Another long pause -

Man Yes, I understand, when he had asked his Uncle about His vision quest the Uncle only replied "you will see when you have your own vision"

Now he understood his Uncle completely.

G/F I too meditated and fasted for three days before you came. Spirits told me a boy/man was coming. I did not know who, just that you were coming.

Silence again - then

G/F Here is my interpretation of your vision. The animal that you saw was like a buffalo but not a Buffalo is called a horse. He will be a great gift to the Cheyenne people when we discover how to use this animal as a creature of burden and a powerful ally in war. It will give us much advantage over the Lakota who we will push to the West into the Black Hills.

You will find a way to do this thing and through it become a great leader to the Great Circle of tribes called the Cheyenne.

Ho - it is spoken.!

The black animal that you saw is a Black Panther not a Mountain Lion as you thought. This animal will give you great power. You must use this power wisely and only for good. Otherwise it will destroy you!

Another long silence

The name you heard is also filled with power, given to you by the Spirits. Do nothing to dishonour your Spirit name.

When the shiver happens to you, you will know that the experience is real. And the information you receive is true. The wolves are your protectors they represent the four directions N E S and W. They too are powerful and provide for your safety as you travel.

The other two animals, the Moose and a Doe each represent something you have been gifted with. The Moose for strength and courage, the

Doe signifies your gentle side, which you may use around children and women that you cross paths with. This is your Female side.

The new self that you felt on standing up after sitting so long is exactly that - your NEW SELF!! It represents growth, strength, resolve and purpose.

The woman that will be your wife will come to you shortly. You will know her when you see her, especially when she walks away from you. She will have an extremely beguiling walk. You will know her immediately.

Boy/Man   Grandfather - I thank you for your interpretations and will hold them in my heart just as you told me to. Please accept my small gifts of a fox fur I captured, killed and cured myself and this basket of wild fruit I picked some days ago. Having spoken Grey Eagle, the new man, strode around the teepee counter clock wise and strode out through the tent flap.

He strode towards the centre of the grand circle to find his Mother and Uncle to tell then some of the things he had learned. His mother would be pleased to know he wished to marry and that she would begin the bargaining process. His Uncle would smile at his progress and future honors. as it was he who had trained his Nephew in all manner of things. He would bring honour to his Uncle.

Ho - it is told. All except one thing.

My name is Grey Eagle and I am a Grandfather now and have told you these things so that you will know who I am.

Ho it is Spoken!!

THE TALE OF
THE CEDAR TREE

As many of you may not know - the Cedar Tree is not native to North America but was imported here from a land called Lebanon - and you may wonder, how did it get here and who brought it.

My name is Grey Eagle and I am here to tell you the story this night.

The last time I spoke to you - I told you a story that had been handed down to the Lakota Sioux by the Elders who told of a Miracle on the Plains. It was the time when TWO WHO WERE ONE spoke to three Medicine Men on the plains. Those who were spoken to were called Runs with Bears, Hunts Wisely and White Cloud. This I know as the tale was handed down to us through the ages by the Story Tellers who were called Twisted Hairs.

The message as spoken by the two who were one was this -.

"Greeting to you three. We bring you good news. This day in a village far away called Bethlehem is born a man-child. He is called Jesus, Emmanuel, and the Great Peacekeeper. To the people of the Plains he shall be called The Dawn Star, Elder Brother, and Pointer of the Way. This shall be the sign to you. He will come bearing a tree that the tribes will use as a healing herb. It will be called Cedar. It will be many seasons before he shall come your way. But come he shall."

Here is how it came about.

It was winter - a time for the Holy Men to remain in their lodgings - sitting quietly - fasting - waiting for messages from the Spirits. Some of the Holy Men waited days for these messages - many of the messages that were given - were not understood by those who received them - often the messages were carried to the Summer rendezvous - told to other Holy Men who would interpret, the messages, These messages were then passed around to the tribes. These visions/messages were shared because they benefited all the tribes as a whole.

This is how it happened:

Again as before, a Wise Man, by the name of Telenka (which means TELLER) in the Lakota language; was driven out of his lodge by a voice telling him to come out on the plains. He was told that he would meet a Man who would change the world and that this man was a Holy Man (Hunkpapa) just as he was. This man would fulfil the prophecy that was given to the Holy Men of the Plains, who were told that the Man would come bearing a gift to the Lakota People. It was the time of fulfillment - it was the time of insights and a time of grace for his tribes and all the other tribes, if they would accept it.

The wise man went out as he was directed because he knew that what the voice was telling him was true. He had heard the voice before and had followed the directions given and had never been wrong. This had lead to his elevated position in the tribe because of his wise counsel.

Winter on the plains, this day was dull, cold but not bitter cold, the sky was laden with clouds, but not stormy because these clouds had not deposited their burden onto the ground. Riding his horse to the east, as he was directed Telenka pondered who he would meet and what it was that he was destined to see. Telenka could see for miles in every direction on the flat rolling plains, but nothing stirred or made its self known to him. He rode for a day, camped in a small hollow that provided some protection from the elements. Built a small fire, fed his horse, ate a small meal and waited. It was always pleasant to be out of the camp for a time, because of the grand silence that was there. The stars were sometimes grand too, but not that night because of the clouds. He wondered what the Spirits had in store for him because the experiences he had had, when he followed the Spirits direction, were always mystifying and satisfying at the same time. What is it this time he mused as he rolled into his blankets and prepared to sleep.

A loud clap of thunder rolled over Telenka's head, but this was winter and it was not supposed to thunder this time of year. He stood up and looked to the East as that is where the faint light of day was visible. Then he heard it, a chanting song, very powerful, sung by many voices. He sharpened his vision, he could see no crowd of people singing a welcome song, a song so strong and so powerful that he felt it clear into his bones. He head vibrated with the power and sweetness of the song. It was if a thousand voices were singing - but nowhere could he see any crowd. Then he saw it, a movement far, far out on the plains. but this was not a crowd of people, as he expected, it appeared to be a lone figure walking. He watched and waited as the lone figure approached him from a great distance. After a time he could make out that the figure was a man, walking toward him. As the figure approached he could see that the man was dressed in white buckskin and carried a curved stick but it was not the curved shape of a coup stick as one would expect, because there were no feathers counting coups, it was just a carved stick of very dark wood, not native to his area. When the figure was a long bow shot away from Telenka he stopped. Then he spoke.

"Greetings Telenka, I come in Peace, I am called Dawn Star, and I bring you greetings from My Sprit Father, who sent me to you and your people."

Telenka returned the greeting and asked, "Are you the one I am supposed to meet?"

"Yes I am." the man replied.

Telenka observed the man in front of him. He was dressed in ceremonial white buckskin with no decorations, the buckskin seemed to glow. The man himself had a strong jaw, dark eyes and long black hair.. His voice was strong and sonorous. He was of medium height and carried himself with authority and inner strength and walked upright as a Warrior would.

"What is it that that you wish to do?"

The man who introduced himself as Dawn Star replied, "I wish you to take me back to your people for I have a story for all and a gift for the People."

Telenka alighted from his horse, gestured to the Man to join him, and began to walk back the way he had come toward the west and the Black Hills visible in the distance.

Together they travelled on foot, for two days. It was a great journey for Telenka as it was a pleasure to be in the Man's company. Often there were no words exchanged, but the presence of the Man, was such that being in his company was enough. The vibrations emanating from the man were soothing in a gentle way, and the exchange between the two travellers was comforting and powerful at the same time.

Telenka thought to himself, "This is a man who is powerful yet he is gentle at the same time. A marvel to be in his presence was all he could think of.

As they approached the village nestled in a grove of trees, Telenka signaled one of the boys on a horse who was guarding the horse herd to come closer. Telenka instructed the boy to ride ahead to the village and tell the Elders that, "He who comes bearing gifts has come as told by the prophecy long ago"

When they arrived at the village, the elders and others were gathered on the edge of the camp waiting respectfully for the arrival of the guest.

Greetings were exchanged by the Elders and the man; he was invited to rest in one of the larger teepees but declined the offer. He said, "I have a story to tell the tribe here and will leave a gift for you and others you come in contact with."

With that he strode to the center of the circle of teepees, sat down and began to speak. A crowd gathered around him from all parts of the camp , women, children, young people and old people, even the dogs, who were generally noisy at the approach of a stranger were strangely silent. As the man spoke his voice carried to all who were near, even some of the people who were absent because of sickness and even the women who were in their Moon Time Lodge, heard him speak.

He said, "I have come so that you may have life and have it more abundantly, I bring you the gift of Peace and Love, so that you may live among your people with joy in your hearts and a song in your total way of life." Be kind to one another, as you would have them be kind to you. Respect your Elders and the ones who gave you life. Help strangers and give to Widows and Orphans so they may live in harmony and without want.

Share what you have so that the welfare of the tribe is your first concern, share knowledge so that the tribe is strengthened by the fostering of knowledge among you all." As he spoke, two small toddlers came out of the crowd and climbed into the Man's lap. "This is another lesson for you all." he said. The children are your most important resource, treat them well and always have their needs foremost in your minds. These children are a most important thing. And so it is where my father dwells, he surrounds himself with his children because the land where he dwells is composed of the minds children."

"A gift I give to you. A tree called cedar, it is medicine for many ills of the People. Your Medicine women will know what to do with the leaves of this tree.

Plant it and nurture it and it will nurture you." With that spoken the Dawn Star placed his hands into a possible sack that no one had noticed he carried. He took out a tree sapling and held it in his hand. He approached the Oldest Elder and handed the cedar sapling to him, after pointing the tree to the four directions in a ceremonial way. The sapling was accepted in a grave manner by the Oldest Elder, who gave a nod of recognition to the giver of the gift. Then he went on to say.

"A sea faring tribe to the north on an Island, did not accept my teachings, they were Hostile to me and what I had to tell them. They tried to kill me, but I passed through them and went away. Other tribes along the sea coast were receptive to my teachings and will prosper greatly. This I say to you, accept my teachings and act on them and you will prosper as well. Follow the ways of the Father Spirit, take counsel with your Elders and prosperity will follow you in this life and also the next." Ho it is spoken.

With those words spoken a chorus of voices could be heard in the sky above the Man's head singing a Joy Song to the Dawn Star and his Father. When the song was finished, the man rose from his seat, walked toward the east. He departed saying, "I go now but I will come back to receive you, so that where I am with my Spirit Father you may be also." I go now to prepare a Lodge for you, so that where I am you may be also." So saying, he turned and walked to the edge of the trees, and disappeared into the forest. Later it was discovered by the Hunters, that he left no tracks, in the woods, but his spirit was always felt among the people.

This is the tale of how the Dawn Star, who was known as Jesus, came to the Lakota People in those days long ago. This is the tale handed down to my people through the ages, to be heard by all who have ears to hear and ears to listen. I Grey Eagle have spoken."

"Ho. It is told."